Honoré de Balzac

The Napoleon of the People; And, The Elixir Of Life

in large print

MEGALI

Honoré de Balzac

The Napoleon of the People; And, The Elixir Of Life

in large print

Reproduction of the original.

1st Edition 2023 | ISBN: 978-3-38731-312-3

Megali Verlag is an imprint of Outlook Verlagsgesellschaft mbH.

Verlag (Publisher): Outlook Verlag GmbH, Zeilweg 44, 60439 Frankfurt, Deutschland
Vertretungsberechtigt (Authorized to represent): E. Roepke, Zeilweg 44, 60439 Frankfurt, Deutschland
Druck (Print): Books on Demand GmbH, In de Tarpen 42, 22848 Norderstedt, Deutschland

THE NAPOLEON OF THE PEOPLE

AND

THE ELIXIR OF LIFE

BY
HONORE DE BALZAC

THE NAPOLEON OF THE PEOPLE

Translated by
Ellen Marriage and Clara Bell.

Napoleon, you see, my friends, was born in Corsica, which is a French island warmed by the Italian sun; it is like a furnace there, everything is scorched up, and they keep on killing each other from father to son for generations all about nothing at all—'tis a notion they have. To begin at the beginning, there was something extraordinary about the thing from the first; it occurred to his mother, who was the handsomest woman of her time, and a shrewd soul, to dedicate him to God, so that he should escape all the dangers of infancy and of his after life; for she had dreamed that the world was on fire on the day he was born. It was a prophecy! So she asked God to protect him, on condition that Napoleon should re-establish His holy religion, which had been thrown to the ground just then. That was the agreement; we shall see what came of it.

Now, do you follow me carefully, and tell me whether what you are about to hear is natural.

It is certain sure that only a man who had had imagination enough to make a mysterious compact would be capable of going further than anybody else, and of passing through volleys of grape-shot and showers of bullets which carried us off like flies, but which had a respect for his head. I myself had particular proof of that at Eylau. I see him yet; he climbs a hillock, takes his field-glass, looks along our lines, and says, "That is going on all right." One of the deep fellows, with a bunch of feathers in his cap, used to plague him a good deal from all accounts, following him about everywhere, even when he was getting his meals. This fellow wants to do something clever, so as soon as the Emperor goes away he takes his place. Oh! swept away in a moment! And this is the last of the bunch of feathers! You understand quite clearly that Napoleon had undertaken to keep his secret to himself. That is why those who accompanied him, and even his especial friends, used to drop like nuts: Duroc, Bessieres, Lannes—men as strong as bars of steel, which he cast into shape for his own ends. And here is a final proof that he was the child of God, created to be the soldier's father; for no one ever saw him as a lieutenant or a captain. He is a commandant straight off! Ah! yes, indeed! He did not look more than four-and-twenty, but he was an old general ever since the taking of Toulon, when he made a beginning by showing the rest that they knew nothing about handling cannon. Next thing he does, he tumbles upon us. A little slip of a general-in-chief of the army of Italy, which had neither bread nor ammunition nor shoes nor clothes—a wretched army as naked as a worm.

"Friends," he said, "here we all are together. Now, get it well into your pates that in a fortnight's time from now you will be the victors, and dressed in new clothes; you shall all have greatcoats, strong gaiters, and famous pairs of shoes; but, my children, you will have to march on Milan to take them, where all these things are."

So they marched. The French, crushed as flat as a pancake, held up their heads again. There were thirty thousand of us tatterdemalions against eighty thousand swaggerers of Germans—fine tall men and well equipped; I can see them yet. Then Napoleon, who was only Bonaparte in those days, breathed goodness knows what into us, and on we marched night and day. We rap their knuckles at Montenotte; we hurry on to thrash them at Rivoli, Lodi, Arcola, and Millesimo, and we never let them go. The army came to have a liking for winning battles. Then Napoleon hems them in on all sides, these German generals did not know where to hide themselves so as to have a little peace and comfort; he drubs them soundly, cribs ten thousand of their men at a time by surrounding them with fifteen hundred Frenchmen, whom he makes to spring up after his fashion, and at last he takes their cannon, victuals, money, ammunition, and everything they have that is worth taking; he pitches them into the water, beats them on the mountains, snaps at them in the air, gobbles them up on the earth, and thrashes them everywhere.

There are the troops in full feather again! For, look you, the Emperor (who, for that matter, was a wit) soon sent for the inhabitant, and told him that he had come there to deliver him. Whereupon the civilian finds us free quarters and makes much of us, so do the women, who showed great discernment. To come to a final end; in Ventose '96, which was at that time what the month of March is now, we had been driven up into a corner of the *Pays des Marmottes*; but after the campaign, lo and behold! we were the masters of Italy, just as Napoleon had prophesied. And in the month of March following, in one year and in two campaigns, he brings us within sight of Vienna; we had made a clean sweep of them. We had gobbled down three armies one after another, and taken the conceit out of four Austrian generals; one of them, an old man who had white hair, had been roasted like a rat in the straw before Mantua. The kings were suing for mercy on their knees. Peace had been won. Could a mere mortal have done that? No. God helped him, that is certain. He distributed himself about like the five loaves in the Gospel, commanded on the battlefield all day, and drew up his plans at night. The sentries always saw him coming; he neither ate nor slept. Therefore, recognizing these prodigies, the soldier adopts him for his father. But, forward!

The other folk there in Paris, seeing all this, say among themselves:

"Here is a pilgrim who appears to take his instructions from Heaven above; he is uncommonly likely to lay a hand on France. We must let him loose on Asia or America, and that, perhaps, will keep him quiet."

The same thing was decreed for him as for Jesus Christ; for, as a matter of fact, they give him orders to go on duty down in Egypt. See his resemblance to the Son of God! That is not all, though. He calls all his fire-eaters about him, all those into whom he had more particularly put the devil, and talks to them in this way:

"My friends, for the time being they are giving us Egypt to stop our mouths. But we will swallow down Egypt in a brace of shakes, just as we swallowed Italy, and private soldiers shall be princes, and shall have broad lands of their own. Forward!"

"Forward, lads!" cry the sergeants.

So we come to Toulon on the way to Egypt. Whereupon the English put to sea with all their fleet. But when we are on board, Napoleon says to us:

"They will not see us: and it is right and proper that you should know henceforward that your general has a star in the sky that guides us and watches over us!"

So said, so done. As we sailed over the sea we took Malta, by way of an orange to quench his thirst for victory, for he was a man who must always be doing something. There we are in Egypt. Well and good. Different orders. The Egyptians, look you, are men who, ever since the world has been the world, have been in the habit of having giants to reign over them, and armies like swarms of ants; because it is a country full of genii and crocodiles, where they have built up pyramids as big as our mountains, the fancy took them to stow their kings under the pyramids, so as to keep them fresh, a thing which mightily pleases them all round out there. Whereupon, as we landed, the Little Corporal said to us:

"My children, the country which you are about to conquer worships a lot of idols which you must respect, because the Frenchman ought to be on good terms with all the world, and fight people without giving annoyance. Get it well into your heads to let everything alone at first; for we shall have it all by and by! and forward!"

So far so good. But all those people had heard a prophecy of Napoleon, under the name of *Kebir Bonaberdis*; a word which in our lingo means, "The Sultan fires a shot," and they feared him like the devil. So the Grand Turk, Asia, and Africa have recourse to magic, and they send a demon against us, named the Mahdi, who it was thought had come down from heaven on a white charger which, like its master was bullet-proof, and the pair of them lived on the air of that part of the world. There are people who have seen them, but for my part I cannot give you any certain informations about them. They were the divinities of Arabia and of the Mamelukes who wished their troopers to believe that the Mahdi had the power of preventing them from dying in battle. They gave out that he was an angel sent down to wage war on Napoleon, and to get back Solomon's seal, part of their paraphernalia which they pretended our general had stolen. You will readily understand that we made them cry peccavi all the same.

Ah, just tell me now how they came to know about that compact of Napoleon's? Was that natural?

They took it into their heads for certain that he commanded the genii, and that he went from place to place like a bird in the twinkling of an eye; and it is a fact that he was everywhere. At length it came about that he carried off a queen of theirs. She was the private property of a Mameluke, who, although he had several more of them, flatly refused to strike a bargain, though "the other" offered all his treasures for her and diamonds as big as pigeon's eggs. When things had come to that pass, they could not well be settled without a good deal of fighting; and there was fighting enough for everybody and no mistake about it.

Then we are drawn up before Alexandria, and again at Gizeh, and before the Pyramids. We had to march over the sands and in the sun; people whose eyes dazzled used to see water that they could not drink and shade that made them fume. But we made short work of the Mamelukes as usual, and everything goes down before the voice of Napoleon, who seizes Upper and Lower Egypt and Arabia, far and wide, till we came to the capitals of kingdoms which no longer existed, where there were thousands and thousands of statues of all the devils in creation, all done to the life, and another curious thing too, any quantity of lizards. A confounded country where any one could have as many acres of land as he wished for as little as he pleased.

While he was busy inland, where he meant to carry out some wonderful ideas of his, the English burn his fleet for him in Aboukir Bay, for they never could do enough to annoy us. But Napoleon, who was respected East and West, and called "My Son" by the Pope, and "My dear Father" by Mahomet's cousin, makes up his mind to have his revenge on England, and to take India in exchange for his fleet. He set out to lead us into Asia, by way of the Red Sea, through a country where there were palaces for halting-places, and nothing but gold and diamonds to pay the troops with, when the Mahdi comes to an understanding with the Plague, and sends it among us to make a break in our victories. Halt! Then every man files off to that parade from which no one comes back on his two feet. The dying soldier cannot take Acre, into which he forces an entrance three times with a warrior's impetuous enthusiasm; the Plague was too strong for us; there was not even time to say "Your servant, sir!" to the Plague. Every man was down with it. Napoleon alone was as fresh as a rose; the whole army saw him drinking in the Plague without it doing him any harm whatever.

There now, my friends, was that natural, do you think?

The Mamelukes, knowing that we were all on the sick-list, want to stop our road; but it was no use trying that nonsense with Napoleon. So he spoke to his familiars, who had tougher skins than the rest:

"Go and clear the road for me."

Junot, who was his devoted friend, and a first-class fighter, only takes a thousand men, and makes a clean sweep of the Pasha's army, which had the impudence to bar our way. Thereupon back we came to Cairo, our headquarters, and now for another story.

Napoleon being out of the country, France allowed the people in Paris to worry the life out of her. They kept back the soldiers' pay and all their linen and clothing, left them to starve, and expected them to lay down law to the universe, without taking any further trouble in the matter. They were idiots of the kind that amuse themselves with chattering instead of setting themselves to knead the dough. So our armies were defeated, France could not keep her frontiers; The Man was not there. I say The Man, look you, because that was how they called him; but it was stuff and nonsense, for he had a star of his own and all his other peculiarities, it was the rest of us that were mere men. He hears this history of France after his famous battle of Aboukir, where with a single division he routed the grand army of the Turks, twenty-five thousand strong, and jostled more than half of them into the sea, rrrah! without losing more than three hundred of his own men. That was his last thunder-clap in Egypt. He said to himself, seeing that all was lost down there, "I know that I am the saviour of France, and to France I must go."

But you must clearly understand that the army did not know of his departure; for if they had, they would have kept him there by force to make him Emperor of the East. So there we all are without him, and in low spirits, for he was the life of us. He leaves Kleber in command, a great watchdog who passed in his checks at Cairo, murdered by an Egyptian whom they put to death by spiking him with a bayonet, which is their way of guillotining people out there; but he suffered so much, that a soldier took pity on the scoundrel and handed his flask to him; and the Egyptian turned up his eyes then and there with all the pleasure in life. But there is not much fun for us about this little affair. Napoleon steps aboard of a little cockleshell, a mere nothing of a skiff, called the *Fortune*, and in the twinkling of an eye, and in the teeth of the English, who were blockading the place with vessels of the line and cruisers and everything that carries canvas, he lands in France for he always had the faculty of taking the sea at a stride. Was that natural? Bah! as soon as he landed at Frejus, it is as good as saying that he has set foot in Paris. Everybody there worships him; but he calls the Government together.

"What have you done to my children, the soldiers?" he says to the lawyers. "You are a set of good-for-nothings who make fools of other people, and feather your own nests at the expense of France. It will not do. I speak in the name of every one who is discontented."

Thereupon they want to put him off and to get rid of him; but not a bit of it! He locks them up in the barracks where they used to argufy and makes them jump out of the windows. Then he makes them follow in his train, and they all become as mute as fishes and supple as tobacco pouches. So he becomes Consul at a blow. He was not the man to doubt the existence of the Supreme Being; he kept his word with Providence, who had kept His promise in earnest; he sets up religion again, and gives back the churches, and they ring the bells for God and Napoleon. So every one is satisfied: *primo* the priests with whom he allows no one to meddle; *segondo*, the merchant folk who carry on their trades without fear of the *rapiamus* of the law that had pressed too heavily on them; *tertio*, the nobles; for people had fallen into an unfortunate habit of putting them to death, and he puts a stop to this.

But there were enemies to be cleared out of the way, and he was not the one to go to sleep after mess; and his eyes, look you, traveled all over the world as if it had been a man's face. The next thing he did was to turn up in Italy; it was just as if he had put his head out of the window and the sight of him was enough; they gulp down the Austrians at Marengo like a whale swallowing gudgeons! *Haouf*! The French Victories blew their trumpets so loud that the whole world could hear the noise, and there was an end of it.

"We will not keep on at this game any longer!" say the Germans.

"That is enough of this sort of thing," say the others.

Here is the upshot. Europe shows the white feather, England knuckles under, general peace all round, and kings and peoples pretending to embrace each other. While then and there the Emperor hits on the idea of the Legion of Honor. There's a fine thing if you like!

He spoke to the whole army at Boulogne. "In France," so he said, "every man is brave. So the civilian who does gloriously shall be the soldier's sister, the soldier shall be his brother, and both shall stand together beneath the flag of honor."

By the time that the rest of us who were away down there in Egypt had come back again, everything was changed. We had seen him last as a general, and in no time we find that he is Emperor! And when this was settled (and it may safely be said that every one was satisfied) there was a holy ceremony such as was never seen under the canopy of heaven. Faith, France gave herself to him, like a handsome girl to a lancer, and the Pope and all his cardinals in robes of red and gold come across the Alps on purpose to anoint him before the army and the people, who clap their hands.

There is one thing that it would be very wrong to keep back from you. While he was in Egypt, in the desert not far away from Syria, *the Red Man* had appeared to him on the mountain of Moses, in order to say, "Everything is going on well." Then again, on the eve of victory at Marengo, the Red Man springs to his feet in front of the Emperor for the second time, and says to him:

"You shall see the world at your feet; you shall be Emperor of the French, King of Italy, master of Holland, ruler of Spain, Portugal, and the Illyrian Provinces, protector of Germany, saviour of Poland, first eagle of the Legion of Honor and all the rest of it."

That Red Man, look you, was a notion of his own, who ran on errands and carried messages, so many people say, between him and his star. I myself have never believed that;

but the Red Man is, undoubtedly, a fact. Napoleon himself spoke of the Red Man who lived up in the roof of the Tuileries, and who used to come to him, he said, in moments of trouble and difficulty. So on the night after his coronation Napoleon saw him for the third time, and they talked over a lot of things together.

Then the Emperor goes straight to Milan to have himself crowned King of Italy, and then came the real triumph of the soldier. For every one who could write became an officer forthwith, and pensions and gifts of duchies poured down in showers. There were fortunes for the staff that never cost France a penny, and the Legion of Honor was as good as an annuity for the rank and file; I still draw my pension on the strength of it. In short, here were armies provided for in a way that had never been seen before! But the Emperor, who knew that he was to be Emperor over everybody, and not only over the army, bethinks himself of the bourgeois, and sets them to build fairy monuments in places that had been as bare as the back of my hand till then. Suppose, now, that you are coming out of Spain and on the way to Berlin; well, you would see triumphal arches, and in the sculpture upon them the common soldiers are done every bit as beautifully as the generals!

In two or three years Napoleon fills his cellars with gold, makes bridges, palaces, roads, scholars, festivals, laws, fleets, and harbors; he spends millions on millions, ever so much, and ever so much more to it, so that I have heard it said that he could have paved the whole of France with five-franc pieces if the fancy had taken him; and all this without putting any taxes on you people here. So when he was comfortably seated on his throne, and so thoroughly the master of the situation, that all Europe was waiting for leave to do anything for him that he might happen to want; as he had four brothers and three sisters, he said to us, just as it might be by way of conversation, in the order of the day:

"Children, is it fitting that your Emperor's relations should beg their bread? No; I want them all to be luminaries, like me in fact! Therefore, it is urgently necessary to conquer a kingdom for each one of them, so that the French nation may be masters everywhere, so that the Guard may make the whole earth tremble, and France may spit wherever she likes, and every nation shall say to her, as it is written on my coins, 'God protects you.'"

"All right!" answers the army, "we will fish up kingdoms for you with the bayonet."

Ah! there was no backing out of it, look you! If he had taken it into his head to conquer the moon, we should have had to put everything in train, pack our knapsacks, and scramble up; luckily, he had no wish for that excursion. The kings who were used to the comforts of a throne, of course, objected to be lugged off, so we had marching orders. We march, we get there, and the earth begins to shake to its centre again. What times they were for wearing out men and shoe-leather! And the hard knocks that they gave us! Only Frenchmen could have stood it. But you are not ignorant that a Frenchman is a born philosopher; he knows that he must die a little sooner or a litter later. So we used to die without a word, because we had the pleasure of watching the Emperor do *this* on the maps.

[Here the soldier swung quickly round on one foot, so as to trace a circle on the barn floor with the other.]

"There, that shall be a kingdom," he used to say, and it was a kingdom. What fine times they were! Colonels became generals whilst you were looking at them, generals became marshals of France, and marshals became kings. There is one of them still left on his feet to keep Europe in mind of those days, Gascon though he may be, and a traitor to France that he might keep his crown; and he did not blush for his shame, for, after all, a crown, look you, is made of gold. The very sappers and miners who knew how to read became great nobles in the same way. And I who am telling you all this have seen in Paris eleven kings and a crowd of princes all round about Napoleon, like rays about the sun! Keep this well in your minds, that as every soldier stood a chance of having a throne of his own (provided he showed himself worthy of it), a corporal of the Guard was by way of being a sight to see, and they gaped at him as he went by; for every one came by his share after a victory, it was made perfectly clear in the bulletin. And what battles they were! Austerlitz, where the army was manoeuvred as if it had been a review; Eylau, where the Russians were drowned in a lake, just as if Napoleon had breathed on them and blown them in; Wagram, where the fighting was kept up for three whole days without flinching. In short, there were as many battles as there are saints in the calendar.

Then it was made clear beyond a doubt that Napoleon bore the Sword of God in his scabbard. He had a regard for the soldier. He took the soldier for his child. He was anxious that you should have shoes, shirts, greatcoats, bread, and cartridges; but he kept up his majesty, too, for reigning was his own particular occupation. But, all the same, a sergeant, or even a common soldier, could go up to him and call him "Emperor," just as you might say "My good friend" to me at times. And he would give an answer to anything you put before him. He used to sleep on the snow just like the rest of us—in short, he looked almost like an ordinary man; but I who am telling you all these things have seen him myself with the grape-shot whizzing about his ears, no more put out by it than you are at this moment; never moving a limb, watching through his field-glass, always looking after his business; so we stood our ground likewise, as cool and calm as John the Baptist. I do not know how he did it; but whenever he spoke, a something in his words made our hearts burn within us; and just to let him see that we were his children, and that it was not in us to shirk or flinch, we used to walk just as usual right up to the sluts of cannon that were belching smoke and vomiting battalions of balls, and never a man would so much as say, "Look out!" It was a something that made dying men raise their heads to salute him and cry, "Long live the Emperor!"

Was that natural? Would you have done this for a mere man?

Thereupon, having fitted up all his family, and things having so turned out that the Empress Josephine (a good woman for all that) had no children, he was obliged to part company with her, although he loved her not a little. But he must have children, for reasons of State. All the crowned heads of Europe, when they heard of his difficulty, squabbled among themselves as to who should find him a wife. He married an Austrian princess, so they say, who was the daughter of the Caesars, a man of antiquity whom everybody talks about, not only in our country, where it is said that most things were his doing, but also all over Europe. And so certain sure is that, that I who am talking to you have been myself across the Danube, where I saw the ruins of a bridge built by that man; and it appeared that he was some connection of Napoleon's at Rome, for the Emperor claimed succession there for his son.

So, after his wedding, which was a holiday for the whole world, and when they let the people off their taxes for ten years to come (though they had to pay them just the same after all, because the excisemen took no notice of the proclamation)—after his wedding, I say, his wife had a child who was King of Rome; a child was born a King while his father was alive, a thing that had never been seen in the world before! That day a balloon set out from Paris to carry the news to Rome, and went all the way in one day. There, now! Is there one of you who will stand me out that there was nothing supernatural in that? No, it was decreed on high. And the mischief take those who will not allow that it was wafted over by God Himself, so as to add to the honor and glory of France!

But there was the Emperor of Russia, a friend of our Emperor's, who was put out because he had not married a Russian lady. So the Russian backs up our enemies the English; for there had always been something to prevent Napoleon from putting a spoke in their wheel. Clearly an end must be made of fowl of that feather. Napoleon is vexed, and he says to us:

"Soldiers! You have been the masters of every capital in Europe, except Moscow, which is allied to England. So, in order to conquer London and India, which belongs to them in London, I find it absolutely necessary that we go to Moscow."

Thereupon the greatest army that ever wore gaiters, and left its footprints all over the globe, is brought together, and drawn up with such peculiar cleverness, that the Emperor passed a million men in review, all in a single day.

"Hourra!" cry the Russians, and there is all Russia assembled, a lot of brutes of Cossacks, that you never can come up with! It was country against country, a general stramash; we had to look out for ourselves. "It was all Asia against Europe," as the Red Man had said to Napoleon. "All right," Napoleon had answered, "I shall be ready for them."

And there, in fact, were all the kings who came to lick Napoleon's hand. Austria, Prussia, Bavaria, Saxony, Poland, and Italy, all speaking us fair and going along with us; it was a fine thing! The Eagles had never cooed before as they did on parade in those days, when they were reared above all the flags of all the nations of Europe. The Poles could not contain their joy because the Emperor had a notion of setting up their kingdom again; and ever since Poland and France have always been like brothers. In short, the army shouts, "Russia shall be ours!"

We cross the frontiers, all the lot of us. We march and better march, but never a Russian do we see. At last all our watch-dogs are encamped at Borodino. That was where I received the Cross, and there is no denying that it was a cursed battle. The Emperor was not easy in his mind; he had seen the Red Man, who said to him, "My child, you are going a little too fast for your feet; you will run short of men, and your friends will play you false."

Thereupon the Emperor proposes a treaty. But before he signs it, he says to us:

"Let us give these Russians a drubbing!"

"All right!" cried the army.

"Forward!" say the sergeants.

My clothes were all falling to pieces, my shoes were worn out with trapezing over those roads out there, which are not good going at all. But it is all one. "Since here is the last of the row," said I to myself, "I mean to get all I can out of it."

We were posted before the great ravine; we had seats in the front row. The signal is given, and seven hundred guns begin a conversation fit to make the blood spirt from your ears. One should give the devil his due, and the Russians let themselves be cut in pieces just like Frenchmen; they did not give way, and we made no advance.

"Forward!" is the cry; "here is the Emperor!"

So it was. He rides past us at a gallop, and makes a sign to us that a great deal depends on our carrying the redoubt. He puts fresh heart into us; we rush forward, I am the first man to reach the gorge. Ah! *mon Dieu*! how they fell, colonels, lieutenants, and common soldiers, all alike! There were shoes to fit up those who had none, and epaulettes for the knowing fellows that knew how to write.... Victory is the cry all along the line! And, upon my word, there were twenty-five thousand Frenchmen lying on the field. No more, I assure you! Such a thing was never seen before, it was just like a field when the corn is cut, with a man lying there for every ear of corn. That sobered the rest of us. The Man comes, and we make a circle round about him, and he coaxes us round (for he could be very nice when he chose), and persuades us to dine with Duke Humphrey, when we were hungry as hunters. Then our consoler distributes the Crosses of the Legion of Honor himself, salutes the dead, and says to us, "On to Moscow!"

"To Moscow, so be it," says the army.

We take Moscow. What do the Russians do but set fire to their city! There was a blaze, two leagues of bonfire that burned for two days! The buildings fell about our ears like slates, and molten lead and iron came down in showers; it was really horrible; it was a light to see our sorrows by, I can tell you! The Emperor said, "There, that is enough of this sort of thing; all my men shall stay here."

We amuse ourselves for a bit by recruiting and repairing our frames, for we really were much fatigued by the campaign. We take away with us a gold cross from the top of the Kremlin, and every soldier had a little fortune. But on the way back the winter came down on us a month earlier than usual, a matter which the learned (like a set of fools) have never sufficiently explained; and we are nipped with the cold. We were no longer an army after that, do you understand? There was an end of generals and even of the sergeants; hunger and misery took the command instead, and all of us were absolutely equal under their reign. All we thought of was how to get back to France; no one stooped to pick up his gun or his money; every one walked straight before him, and armed himself as he thought fit, and no one cared about glory.

The Emperor saw nothing of his star all the time, for the weather was so bad. There was some misunderstanding between him and heaven. Poor man, how bad he felt when he saw his Eagles flying with their backs turned on victory! That was really too rough! Well, the next thing is the Beresina. And here and now, my friends, any one can assure you on his honor, and by all that is sacred, that *never*, no, never since there have been men on earth, never in this world has there been such a fricasse of an army, caissons, transports, artillery and all, in such snow as that and under such a pitiless sky. It was so cold that you burned your hand on the barrel of your gun if you happened to touch it. There it was that the pontooners saved the army, for the pontooners stood firm at their posts; it was there that Gondrin behaved like a hero, and he is the sole survivor of all the men who were dogged enough to stand in the river so as to build the bridges on which the army crossed over, and so escaped the Russians, who still respected the Grand Army on account of its past victories. And Gondrin is an accomplished soldier, [pointing at Gondrin, who was gazing at him with the rapt attention peculiar to deaf people] a distinguished soldier who deserves to have your very highest esteem.

I saw the Emperor standing by the bridge, and never feeling the cold at all. Was that, again, a natural thing? He was looking on at the loss of his treasures, of his friends, and those who had fought with him in Egypt. Bah! there was an end of everything. Women and wagons and guns were all engulfed and swallowed up, everything went to wreck and ruin. A few of the bravest among us saved the Eagles, for the Eagles, look you, meant France, and all the rest of you; it was the civil and military honor of France that was in our keeping, there must be no spot on the honor of France, and the cold could never make her bow her head. There was no getting warm except in the neighborhood of the Emperor; for whenever he was in danger we hurried up, all frozen as we were—we who would not stop to hold out a hand to a fallen friend.

They say, too, that he shed tears of a night over his poor family of soldiers. Only he and Frenchmen could have pulled themselves out of such a plight; but we did pull ourselves out, though, as I am telling you, it was with loss, ay, and heavy loss. The Allies had eaten up all our provisions; everybody began to betray him, just as the Red Man had foretold. The rattle-pates in Paris, who had kept quiet ever since the Imperial Guard had been established, think that *he* is dead, and hatch a conspiracy. They set to work in the Home Office to overturn the Emperor. These things come to his knowledge and worry him; he says to us at parting, "Good-bye, children; keep to your posts, I will come back again."

Bah! Those generals of his lose their heads at once; for when he was away, it was not like the same thing. The marshals fall out among themselves, and make blunders, as was only natural, for Napoleon in his kindness had fed them on gold till they had grown as fat as butter, and they had no mind to march. Troubles came of this, for many of them stayed inactive in garrison towns in the rear, without attempting to tickle up the backs of the enemy behind us, and we were being driven back on France. But Napoleon comes back among us with fresh troops; conscripts they were, and famous conscripts too; he had put some thorough notions of discipline into them—the whelps were good to set their teeth in anybody. He had a bourgeois guard of honor too, and fine troops they were! They melted away like butter on a gridiron. We may put a bold front on it, but everything is against us, although the army still performs prodigies of valor. Whole nations fought against nations in tremendous battles, at Dresden, Lutzen, and Bautzen, and then it was that France showed extraordinary heroism, for you must all of you bear in mind that in those times a stout grenadier only lasted six months.

We always won the day, but the English were always on our track, putting nonsense into other nations' heads, and stirring them up to revolt. In short, we cleared a way through all these mobs of nations; for wherever the Emperor appeared, we made a passage for him; for on the land as on the sea, whenever he said, "I wish to go forward," we made the way.

There comes a final end to it at last. We are back in France; and in spite of the bitter weather, it did one's heart good to breathe one's native air again, it set up many a poor fellow; and as for me, it put new life into me, I can tell you. But it was a question all at once of defending France, our fair land of France. All Europe was up in arms against us; they took it in bad part that we had tried to keep the Russians in order by driving them back within their own borders, so that they should not gobble us up, for those Northern folk have a strong liking for eating up the men of the South, it is a habit they have; I have heard the same thing of them from several generals.

So the Emperor finds his own father-in-law, his friends whom he had made crowned kings, and the rabble of princes to whom he had given back their thrones, were all against him. Even Frenchmen and allies in our own ranks turned against us, by orders from high quarters, as at Leipsic. Common soldiers would hardly be capable of such abominations; yet these princes, as they called themselves, broke their words three times a day! The next thing they do is to invade France. Wherever our Emperor shows his lion's face, the enemy beats a retreat; he worked more miracles for the defence of France than he had ever wrought in the conquest of Italy, the East, Spain, Europe, and Russia; he has a mind to bury every foreigner in French soil, to give them a respect for France, so he lets them come close up to Paris, so as to do for them at a single blow, and to rise to the highest height of genius in the biggest battle that ever was fought, a mother of battles! But the Parisians wanting to save their trumpery skins, and afraid for their twopenny shops, open their gates and there is a beginning of the *ragusades*, and an end of all joy and happiness; they make a fool of the Empress, and fly the white flag out at the windows. The Emperor's closest friends among his generals forsake him at last and go over to the Bourbons, of whom no one had ever heard tell. Then he bids us farewell at Fontainebleau:

"Soldiers!"... I can hear him yet, we were all crying just like children; the Eagles and the flags had been lowered as if for a funeral. Ah! and it was a funeral, I can tell you; it was the funeral of the Empire; those smart armies of his were nothing but skeletons now. So he stood there on the flight of steps before his chateau, and he said:

"Children, we have been overcome by treachery, but we shall meet again up above in the country of the brave. Protect my child, I leave him in your care. *Long live Napoleon II.!*"

He had thought of killing himself, so that no one should behold Napoleon after his defeat; like Jesus Christ before the Crucifixion, he thought himself forsaken by God and by his talisman, and so he took enough poison to kill a regiment, but it had no effect whatever upon him. Another marvel! he discovered that he was immortal; and feeling sure of his case, and knowing that he would be Emperor for ever, he went to an island for a little while, so as to study the dispositions of those folk who did not fail to make blunder upon blunder. Whilst he was biding his time, the Chinese and the brutes out in Africa, the Moors and what-not, awkward customers all of them, were so convinced that he was something more than mortal, that they respected his flag, saying that God would be displeased if any one meddled with it. So he reigned over all the rest of the world, although the doors of his own France had been closed upon him.

Then he goes on board the same nutshell of a skiff that he sailed in from Egypt, passes under the noses of the English vessels, and sets foot in France. France recognizes her Emperor, the cuckoo flits from steeple to steeple; France cries with one voice, "Long live the Emperor!" The enthusiasm for that Wonder of the Ages was thoroughly genuine in these parts. Dauphine behaved handsomely; and I was uncommonly pleased to learn that people here shed tears of joy on seeing his gray overcoat once more.

It was on March 1st that Napoleon set out with two hundred men to conquer the kingdom of France and Navarre, which by March 20th had become the French Empire again. On that day he found himself in Paris, and a clean sweep had been made of everything; he had won back his beloved France, and had called all his soldiers about him again, and three words of his had done it all—"Here am I!" 'Twas the greatest miracle God ever worked! Was it ever known in the world before that a man should do nothing but show his hat, and a whole Empire became his? They fancied that France was crushed, did they? Never a bit of it. A National Army springs up again at the sight of the Eagle, and we all march to Waterloo. There the Guard fall all as one man. Napoleon in his despair heads the rest, and flings himself three times on the enemy's guns without finding the death he sought; we all saw him do it, we soldiers, and the day was lost! That night the Emperor calls all his old soldiers about him, and there on the battlefield, which was soaked with our blood, he burns his flags and his Eagles—the poor Eagles that had never been defeated, that had cried, "Forward!" in battle after battle, and had flown above us all over Europe. That was the end of the Eagles—all the wealth of England could not purchase for her one tail-feather. The rest is sufficiently known.

The Red Man went over to the Bourbons like the low scoundrel he is. France is prostrate, the soldier counts for nothing, they rob him of his due, send him about his business, and fill his place with nobles who could not walk, they were so old, so that it made you sorry to see them. They seize Napoleon by treachery, the English shut him up on a desert island in the ocean, on a rock ten thousand feet above the rest of the world. That is the final end of it; there he has to stop till the Red Man gives him back his power again, for the happiness of France. A lot of them say that he is dead! Dead? Oh! yes, very likely. They do not know him, that is plain! They go on telling that fib to deceive the people, and to keep things quiet for their tumble-down government. Listen; this is the whole truth of the matter. His friends have left him alone in the desert to fulfil a prophecy that was made about him, for I forgot to tell you that his name Napoleon really means the *Lion of the Desert*. And that is gospel truth. You will hear plenty of other things said about the Emperor, but they are all monstrous nonsense. Because, look you, to no

man of woman born would God have given the power to
write his name in red, as he did, across the earth, where he
will be remembered for ever!... Long live "Napoleon, the
father of the soldier, the father of the people!"

THE ELIXIR OF LIFE

TO THE READER

At the very outset of the writer's literary career, a friend, long since dead, gave him the subject of this Study. Later on he found the same story in a collection published about the beginning of the present century. To the best of his belief, it is some stray fancy of the brain of Hoffmann of Berlin; probably it appeared in some German almanac, and was omitted in the published editions of his collected works. The *Comedie Humaine* is sufficiently rich in original creations for the author to own to this innocent piece of plagiarism; when, like the worthy La Fontaine, he has told unwittingly, and after his own fashion, a tale already related by another. This is not one of the hoaxes in vogue in the year 1830, when every author wrote his "tale of horror" for the amusement of young ladies. When you have read the account of Don Juan's decorous parricide, try to picture to yourself the part which would be played under very similar circumstances by honest folk who, in this nineteenth century, will take a man's money and undertake to pay him a life annuity on the faith of a chill, or let a house to an ancient lady for the term of her natural life! Would they be for resuscitating their clients? I should dearly like a connoisseur in consciences to consider how far there is a resemblance between a Don Juan and fathers who marry their children to great expectations. Does humanity, which, according to certain philosophers, is making progress, look on the art of waiting for dead men's shoes as a step in the right direction? To this art we owe several honorable professions, which open up ways of living on death. There are people who rely entirely on an expected demise; who brood over it, crouching each morning upon a corpse, that serves again for their pillow at night. To this class belong bishops' coadjutors, cardinals' supernumeraries, *tontiniers*, and the like. Add to the list many delicately scrupulous persons eager to buy landed property beyond their means, who calculate with dry logic and in cold blood the probable duration of the life of a father or of a step-mother, some old man or woman of eighty or ninety, saying to themselves, "I shall be sure to come in for it in three years' time, and then——" A murderer is less loathsome to us than a spy. The murderer may have acted on a sudden mad impulse; he may be penitent and amend; but a spy is always a spy, night and day, in bed, at table, as he walks abroad; his vileness pervades every moment of his life. Then what must it be to live when every moment of your life is tainted with murder? And have we not just admitted that a host of human creatures in our midst are led by our laws, customs, and usages to dwell without ceasing on a fellow-creature's death? There are men who put the weight of a coffin into their deliberations as they bargain for Cashmere shawls for their wives, as they go up the staircase of a theatre, or think of going to the Bouffons, or of setting up a carriage; who are murderers in thought when dear ones, with the irresistible charm of innocence, hold up childish foreheads to be kissed with a "Good-night, father!" Hourly they meet the gaze of eyes that they would fain close for ever, eyes that still open each morning to the light, like Belvidero's in this Study. God alone knows the number of those who are parricides in thought. Picture to yourself the state of mind of a man who must pay a life annuity to some old woman whom he scarcely knows; both live in the country with a brook between them, both sides are free to hate cordially, without offending against the social conventions that require two brothers to wear a mask if the older will succeed to the entail, and the other to the fortune of a younger son. The whole civilization of Europe turns upon the principle of hereditary succession as upon a pivot; it would be madness to subvert the principle; but could we not, in an age that prides itself upon its mechanical inventions, perfect this essential portion of the social machinery?

If the author has preserved the old-fashioned style of address *To the Reader* before a work wherein he endeavors to represent all literary forms, it is for the purpose of making a remark that applies to several of the Studies, and very specially to this. Every one of his compositions has been based upon ideas more or less novel, which, as it seemed to him, needed literary expression; he can claim priority for certain forms and for certain ideas which have since passed into the domain of literature, and have there, in some instances, become common property; so that the date of the first publication of each Study cannot be a matter of indifference to those of his readers who would fain do him justice.

Reading brings us unknown friends, and what friend is like a reader? We have friends in our own circle who read nothing of ours. The author hopes to pay his debt, by dedicating this work *Diis ignotis.*

THE ELIXIR OF LIFE

Translated By Clara Bell and
James Waring

One winter evening, in a princely palace at Ferrara, Don Juan Belvidero was giving a banquet to a prince of the house of Este. A banquet in those times was a marvelous spectacle which only royal wealth or the power of a mightly [sic] lord could furnish forth. Seated about a table lit up with perfumed tapers, seven laughter-loving women were interchanging sweet talk. The white marble of the noble works of art about them stood out against the red stucco walls, and made strong contrasts with the rich Turkey carpets. Clad in satin, glittering with gold, and covered with gems less brilliant than their eyes, each told a tale of energetic passions as diverse as their styles of beauty. They differed neither in their ideas nor in their language; but the expression of their eyes, their glances, occasional gestures, or the tones of their voices supplied a commentary, dissolute, wanton, melancholy, or satirical, to their words.

One seemed to be saying—"The frozen heart of age might kindle at my beauty."

Another—"I love to lounge upon cushions, and think with rapture of my adorers."

A third, a neophyte at these banquets, was inclined to blush. "I feel remorse in the depths of my heart! I am a Catholic, and afraid of hell. But I love you, I love you so that I can sacrifice my hereafter to you."

The fourth drained a cup of Chian wine. "Give me a joyous life!" she cried; "I begin life afresh each day with the dawn. Forgetful of the past, with the intoxication of yesterday's rapture still upon me, I drink deep of life—a whole lifetime of pleasure and of love!"

The woman who sat next to Juan Belvidero looked at him with a feverish glitter in her eyes. She was silent. Then—"I should need no hired bravo to kill my lover if he forsook me!" she cried at last, and laughed, but the marvelously wrought gold comfit box in her fingers was crushed by her convulsive clutch.

"When are you to be Grand Duke?" asked the sixth. There was the frenzy of a Bacchante in her eyes, and her teeth gleamed between the lips parted with a smile of cruel glee.

"Yes, when is that father of yours going to die?" asked the seventh, throwing her bouquet at Don Juan with bewitching playfulness. It was a childish girl who spoke, and the speaker was wont to make sport of sacred things.

"Oh! don't talk about it," cried Don Juan, the young and handsome giver of the banquet. "There is but one eternal father, and, as ill luck will have it, he is mine."

The seven Ferrarese, Don Juan's friends, the Prince himself, gave a cry of horror. Two hundred years later, in the days of Louis XV., people of taste would have laughed at this witticism. Or was it, perhaps, that at the outset of an orgy there is a certain unwonted lucidity of mind? Despite the taper light, the clamor of the senses, the gleam of gold and silver, the fumes of wine, and the exquisite beauty of the women, there may perhaps have been in the depths of the revelers' hearts some struggling glimmer of reverence for things divine and human, until it was drowned in glowing floods of wine! Yet even then the flowers had been crushed, eyes were growing dull, and drunkenness, in Rabelais' phrase, had "taken possession of them down to their sandals."

During that brief pause a door opened; and as once the Divine presence was revealed at Belshazzar's feast, so now it seemed to be manifest in the apparition of an old white-haired servant, who tottered in, and looked sadly from under knitted brows at the revelers. He gave a withering glance at the garlands, the golden cups, the pyramids of fruit, the dazzling lights of the banquet, the flushed scared faces, the hues of the cushions pressed by the white arms of the women.

"My lord, your father is dying!" he said; and at those solemn words, uttered in hollow tones, a veil of crape seemed to be drawn over the wild mirth.

Don Juan rose to his feet with a gesture to his guests that might be rendered by, "Excuse me; this kind of thing does not happen every day."

Does it so seldom happen that a father's death surprises youth in the full-blown splendor of life, in the midst of the mad riot of an orgy? Death is as unexpected in his caprice as a courtesan in her disdain; but death is truer—Death has never forsaken any man.

Don Juan closed the door of the banqueting-hall; and as he went down the long gallery, through the cold and darkness, he strove to assume an expression in keeping with the part he had to play; he had thrown off his mirthful mood, as he had thrown down his table napkin, at the first thought of this role. The night was dark. The mute servitor, his guide to the chamber where the dying man lay, lighted the way so dimly that Death, aided by cold, silence, and darkness, and it may be by a reaction of drunkenness, could send some sober thoughts through the spendthrift's soul. He examined his life, and became thoughtful, like a man involved in a lawsuit on his way to the Court.

Bartolommeo Belvidero, Don Juan's father, was an old man of ninety, who had devoted the greatest part of his life to business pursuits. He had acquired vast wealth in many a journey to magical Eastern lands, and knowledge, so it was said, more valuable than the gold and diamonds, which had almost ceased to have any value for him.

"I would give more to have a tooth in my head than for a ruby," he would say at times with a smile. The indulgent father loved to hear Don Juan's story of this and that wild freak of youth. "So long as these follies amuse you, dear boy——" he would say laughingly, as he lavished money on his son. Age never took such pleasure in the sight of youth; the fond father did not remember his own decaying powers while he looked on that brilliant young life.

Bartolommeo Belvidero, at the age of sixty, had fallen in love with an angel of peace and beauty. Don Juan had been the sole fruit of this late and short-lived love. For fifteen years the widower had mourned the loss of his beloved Juana; and to this sorrow of age, his son and his numerous household had attributed the strange habits that he had contracted. He had shut himself up in the least comfortable wing of his palace, and very seldom left his apartments; even Don Juan himself must first ask permission before seeing his father. If this hermit, unbound by vows, came or went in his palace or in the streets of Ferrara, he walked as if he were in a dream, wholly engrossed, like a man at strife with a memory, or a wrestler with some thought.

The young Don Juan might give princely banquets, the palace might echo with clamorous mirth, horses pawed the ground in the courtyards, pages quarreled and flung dice upon the stairs, but Bartolommeo ate his seven ounces of bread daily and drank water. A fowl was occasionally dressed for him, simply that the black poodle, his faithful companion, might have the bones. Bartolommeo never complained of the noise. If the huntsmen's horns and baying dogs disturbed his sleep during his illness, he only said, "Ah! Don Juan has come back again." Never on earth has there been a father so little exacting and so indulgent; and, in consequence, young Belvidero, accustomed to treat his father unceremoniously, had all the faults of a spoiled child. He treated old Bartolommeo as a wilful courtesan treats an elderly adorer; buying indemnity for insolence with a smile, selling good-humor, submitting to be loved.

Don Juan, beholding scene after scene of his younger years, saw that it would be a difficult task to find his father's indulgence at fault. Some new-born remorse stirred the depths of his heart; he felt almost ready to forgive this father now about to die for having lived so long. He had an accession of filial piety, like a thief's return in thought to honesty at the prospect of a million adroitly stolen.

Before long Don Juan had crossed the lofty, chilly suite of rooms in which his father lived; the penetrating influences of the damp close air, the mustiness diffused by old tapestries and presses thickly covered with dust had passed into him, and now he stood in the old man's antiquated room, in the repulsive presence of the deathbed, beside a dying fire. A flickering lamp on a Gothic table sent broad uncertain shafts of light, fainter or brighter, across the bed, so that the dying man's face seemed to wear a different look at every moment. The bitter wind whistled through the crannies of the ill-fitting casements; there was a smothered sound of snow lashing the windows. The harsh contrast of these sights and sounds with the scenes which Don Juan had just quitted was so sudden that he could not help shuddering. He turned cold as he came towards the bed; the lamp flared in a sudden vehement gust of wind and lighted up his father's face; the features were wasted and distorted; the skin that cleaved to their bony outlines had taken wan livid hues, all the more ghastly by force of contrast with the white pillows on which he lay. The muscles about the toothless mouth had contracted with pain and drawn apart the lips; the moans that issued between them with appalling energy found an accompaniment in the howling of the storm without.

In spite of every sign of coming dissolution, the most striking thing about the dying face was its incredible power. It was no ordinary spirit that wrestled there with Death. The eyes glared with strange fixity of gaze from the cavernous sockets hollowed by disease. It seemed as if Bartolommeo sought to kill some enemy sitting at the foot of his bed by the intent gaze of dying eyes. That steady remorseless look was the more appalling because the head that lay upon the pillow was passive and motionless as a skull upon a doctor's table. The outlines of the body, revealed by the coverlet, were no less rigid and stiff; he lay there as one dead, save for those eyes. There was something automatic about the moaning sounds that came from the mouth. Don Juan felt something like shame that he must be brought thus to his father's bedside, wearing a courtesan's bouquet, redolent of the fragrance of the banqueting-chamber and the fumes of wine.

"You were enjoying yourself!" the old man cried as he saw his son.

Even as he spoke the pure high notes of a woman's voice, sustained by the sound of the viol on which she accompanied her song, rose above the rattle of the storm against the casements, and floated up to the chamber of death. Don Juan stopped his ears against the barbarous answer to his father's speech.

"I bear you no grudge, my child," Bartolommeo went on.

The words were full of kindness, but they hurt Don Juan; he could not pardon this heart-searching goodness on his father's part.

"What a remorseful memory for me!" he cried, hypocritically.

"Poor Juanino," the dying man went on, in a smothered voice, "I have always been so kind to you, that you could not surely desire my death?"

"Oh, if it were only possible to keep you here by giving up a part of my own life!" cried Don Juan.

("We can always *say* this sort of thing," the spendthrift thought; "it is as if I laid the whole world at my mistress' feet.")

The thought had scarcely crossed his mind when the old poodle barked. Don Juan shivered; the response was so intelligent that he fancied the dog must have understood him.

"I was sure that I could count upon you, my son!" cried the dying man. "I shall live. So be it; you shall be satisfied. I shall live, but without depriving you of a single day of your life."

"He is raving," thought Don Juan. Aloud he added, "Yes, dearest father, yes; you shall live, of course, as long as I live, for your image will be for ever in my heart."

"It is not that kind of life that I mean," said the old noble, summoning all his strength to sit up in bed; for a thrill of doubt ran through him, one of those suspicions that come into being under a dying man's pillow. "Listen, my son," he went on, in a voice grown weak with that last effort, "I have no more wish to give up life than you to give up wine and mistresses, horses and hounds, and hawks and gold——"

"I can well believe it," thought the son; and he knelt down by the bed and kissed Bartolommeo's cold hands. "But, father, my dear father," he added aloud, "we must submit to the will of God."

"I am God!" muttered the dying man.

"Do not blaspheme!" cried the other, as he saw the menacing expression on his father's face. "Beware what you say; you have received extreme unction, and I should be inconsolable if you were to die before my eyes in mortal sin."

"Will you listen to me?" cried Bartolommeo, and his mouth twitched.

Don Juan held his peace; an ugly silence prevailed. Yet above the muffled sound of the beating of the snow against the windows rose the sounds of the beautiful voice and the viol in unison, far off and faint as the dawn. The dying man smiled.

"Thank you," he said, "for bringing those singing voices and the music, a banquet, young and lovely women with fair faces and dark tresses, all the pleasure of life! Bid them wait for me; for I am about to begin life anew."

"The delirium is at its height," said Don Juan to himself.

"I have found out a way of coming to life again," the speaker went on. "There, just look in that table drawer, press the spring hidden by the griffin, and it will fly open."

"I have found it, father."

"Well, then, now take out a little phial of rock crystal."

"I have it."

"I have spent twenty years in——" but even as he spoke the old man felt how very near the end had come, and summoned all his dying strength to say, "As soon as the breath is out of me, rub me all over with that liquid, and I shall come to life again."

"There is very little of it," his son remarked.

Though Bartolommeo could no longer speak, he could still hear and see. When those words dropped from Don Juan, his head turned with appalling quickness, his neck was twisted like the throat of some marble statue which the sculptor had condemned to remain stretched out for ever, the wide eyes had come to have a ghastly fixity.

He was dead, and in death he lost his last and sole illusion.

He had sought a shelter in his son's heart, and it had proved to be a sepulchre, a pit deeper than men dig for their dead. The hair on his head had risen and stiffened with horror, his agonized glance still spoke. He was a father rising in just anger from his tomb, to demand vengeance at the throne of God.

"There! it is all over with the old man!" cried Don Juan.

He had been so interested in holding the mysterious phial to the lamp, as a drinker holds up the wine-bottle at the end of a meal, that he had not seen his father's eyes fade. The cowering poodle looked from his master to the elixir, just as Don Juan himself glanced again and again from his father to the flask. The lamplight flickered. There was a deep silence; the viol was mute. Juan Belvidero thought that he saw his father stir, and trembled. The changeless gaze of those accusing eyes frightened him; he closed them hastily, as he would have closed a loose shutter swayed by the wind of an autumn night. He stood there motionless, lost in a world of thought.

Suddenly the silence was broken by a shrill sound like the creaking of a rusty spring. It startled Don Juan; he all but dropped the phial. A sweat, colder than the blade of a dagger, issued through every pore. It was only a piece of clockwork, a wooden cock that sprang out and crowed three times, an ingenious contrivance by which the learned of that epoch were wont to be awakened at the appointed hour to begin the labors of the day. Through the windows there came already a flush of dawn. The thing, composed of wood, and cords, and wheels, and pulleys, was more faithful in its service than he in his duty to Bartolommeo—he, a man with that peculiar piece of human mechanism within him that we call a heart.

Don Juan the sceptic shut the flask again in the secret drawer in the Gothic table—he meant to run no more risks of losing the mysterious liquid.

Even at that solemn moment he heard the murmur of a crowd in the gallery, a confused sound of voices, of stifled laughter and light footfalls, and the rustling of silks—the sounds of a band of revelers struggling for gravity. The door opened, and in came the Prince and Don Juan's friends, the seven courtesans, and the singers, disheveled and wild like dancers surprised by the dawn, when the tapers that have burned through the night struggle with the sunlight.

They had come to offer the customary condolence to the young heir.

"Oho! is poor Don Juan really taking this seriously?" said the Prince in Brambilla's ear.

"Well, his father was very good," she returned.

But Don Juan's night-thoughts had left such unmistakable traces on his features, that the crew was awed into silence. The men stood motionless. The women, with wine-parched lips and cheeks marbled with kisses, knelt down and began a prayer. Don Juan could scarce help trembling when he saw splendor and mirth and laughter and song and youth and beauty and power bowed in reverence before Death. But in those times, in that adorable Italy of the sixteenth century, religion and revelry went hand in hand; and religious excess became a sort of debauch, and a debauch a religious rite!

The Prince grasped Don Juan's hand affectionately, then when all faces had simultaneously put on the same grimace—half-gloomy, half-indifferent—the whole masque disappeared, and left the chamber of death empty. It was like an allegory of life.

As they went down the staircase, the Prince spoke to Rivabarella: "Now, who would have taken Don Juan's impiety for a boast? He loves his father."

"Did you see that black dog?" asked La Brambilla.

"He is enormously rich now," sighed Bianca Cavatolino.

"What is that to me?" cried the proud Veronese (she who had crushed the comfit-box).

"What does it matter to you, forsooth?" cried the Duke. "With his money he is as much a prince as I am."

At first Don Juan was swayed hither and thither by countless thoughts, and wavered between two decisions. He took counsel with the gold heaped up by his father, and returned in the evening to the chamber of death, his whole soul brimming over with hideous selfishness. He found all his household busy there. "His lordship" was to lie in state to-morrow; all Ferrara would flock to behold the wonderful spectacle; and the servants were busy decking the room and the couch on which the dead man lay. At a sign from Don Juan all his people stopped, dumfounded and trembling.

"Leave me alone here," he said, and his voice was changed, "and do not return until I leave the room."

When the footsteps of the old servitor, who was the last to go, echoed but faintly along the paved gallery, Don Juan hastily locked the door, and sure that he was quite alone, "Let us try," he said to himself.

Bartolommeo's body was stretched on a long table. The embalmers had laid a sheet over it, to hide from all eyes the dreadful spectacle of a corpse so wasted and shrunken that it seemed like a skeleton, and only the face was uncovered. This mummy-like figure lay in the middle of the room. The limp clinging linen lent itself to the outlines it shrouded—so sharp, bony, and thin. Large violet patches had already begun to spread over the face; the embalmers' work had not been finished too soon.

Don Juan, strong as he was in his scepticism, felt a tremor as he opened the magic crystal flask. When he stood over that face, he was trembling so violently, that he was actually obliged to wait for a moment. But Don Juan had acquired an early familiarity with evil; his morals had been corrupted by a licentious court, a reflection worthy of the Duke of Urbino crossed his mind, and it was a keen sense of curiosity that goaded him into boldness. The devil himself might have whispered the words that were echoing through his brain, *Moisten one of the eyes with the liquid*! He took up a linen cloth, moistened it sparingly with the precious fluid, and passed it lightly over the right eyelid of the corpse. The eye unclosed....

"Aha!" said Don Juan. He gripped the flask tightly, as we clutch in dreams the branch from which we hang suspended over a precipice.

For the eye was full of life. It was a young child's eye set in a death's head; the light quivered in the depths of its youthful liquid brightness. Shaded by the long dark lashes, it sparkled like the strange lights that travelers see in lonely places in winter nights. The eye seemed as if it would fain dart fire at Don Juan; he saw it thinking, upbraiding, condemning, uttering accusations, threatening doom; it cried aloud, and gnashed upon him. All anguish that shakes human souls was gathered there; supplications the most tender, the wrath of kings, the love in a girl's heart pleading with the headsman; then, and after all these, the deeply searching glance a man turns on his fellows as he mounts the last step of the scaffold. Life so dilated in this fragment of life that Don

Juan shrank back; he walked up and down the room, he dared not meet that gaze, but he saw nothing else. The ceiling and the hangings, the whole room was sown with living points of fire and intelligence. Everywhere those gleaming eyes haunted him.

"He might very likely have lived another hundred years!" he cried involuntarily. Some diabolical influence had drawn him to his father, and again he gazed at that luminous spark. The eyelid closed and opened again abruptly; it was like a woman's sign of assent. It was an intelligent movement. If a voice had cried "Yes!" Don Juan could not have been more startled.

"What is to be done?" he thought.

He nerved himself to try to close the white eyelid. In vain.

"Kill it? That would perhaps be parricide," he debated with himself.

"Yes," the eye said, with a strange sardonic quiver of the lid.

"Aha!" said Don Juan to himself, "here is witchcraft at work!" And he went closer to crush the thing. A great tear trickled over the hollow cheeks, and fell on Don Juan's hand.

"It is scalding!" he cried. He sat down. The struggle exhausted him; it was as if, like Jacob of old, he was wrestling with an angel.

At last he rose. "So long as there is no blood——" he muttered.

Then, summoning all the courage needed for a coward's crime, he extinguished the eye, pressing it with the linen cloth, turning his head away. A terrible groan startled him. It was the poor poodle, who died with a long-drawn howl.

"Could the brute have been in the secret?" thought Don Juan, looking down at the faithful creature.

Don Juan Belvidero was looked upon as a dutiful son. He reared a white marble monument on his father's tomb, and employed the greatest sculptors of the time upon it. He did not recover perfect ease of mind till the day when his father knelt in marble before Religion, and the heavy weight of the stone had sealed the mouth of the grave in which he had laid the one feeling of remorse that sometimes flitted through his soul in moments of physical weariness.

He had drawn up a list of the wealth heaped up by the old merchant in the East, and he became a miser: had he not to provide for a second lifetime? His views of life were the more profound and penetrating; he grasped its significance, as a whole, the better, because he saw it across a grave. All men, all things, he analyzed once and for all; he summed up the Past, represented by its records; the Present in the law, its crystallized form; the Future, revealed by religion. He took spirit and matter, and flung them into his crucible, and found—Nothing. Thenceforward he became DON JUAN.

At the outset of his life, in the prime of youth and the beauty of youth, he knew the illusions of life for what they were; he despised the world, and made the utmost of the world. His felicity could not have been of the bourgeois kind, rejoicing in periodically recurrent *bouilli*, in the comforts of a warming-pan, a lamp of a night, and a new pair of slippers once a quarter. Nay, rather he seized upon existence as a monkey snatches a nut, and after no long toying with it, proceeds deftly to strip off the mere husks to reach the savory kernel within.

Poetry and the sublime transports of passion scarcely reached ankle-depth with him now. He in nowise fell into the error of strong natures who flatter themselves now and again that little souls will believe in a great soul, and are willing to barter their own lofty thoughts of the future for the small change of our life-annuity ideas. He, even as they, had he chosen, might well have walked with his feet on the earth and his head in the skies; but he liked better to sit on earth, to wither the soft, fresh, fragrant lips of a woman with kisses, for like Death, he devoured everything without scruple as he passed; he would have full fruition; he was an

Oriental lover, seeking prolonged pleasures easily obtained. He sought nothing but a woman in women, and cultivated cynicism, until it became with him a habit of mind. When his mistress, from the couch on which she lay, soared and was lost in regions of ecstatic bliss, Don Juan followed suit, earnest, expansive, serious as any German student. But he said I, while she, in the transports of intoxication, said We. He understood to admiration the art of abandoning himself to the influence of a woman; he was always clever enough to make her believe that he trembled like some boy fresh from college before his first partner at a dance, when he asks her, "Do you like dancing?" But, no less, he could be terrible at need, could unsheathe a formidable sword and make short work of Commandants. Banter lurked beneath his simplicity, mocking laughter behind his tears—for he had tears at need, like any woman nowadays who says to her husband, "Give me a carriage, or I shall go into a consumption."

For the merchant the world is a bale of goods or a mass of circulating bills; for most young men it is a woman, and for a woman here and there it is a man; for a certain order of mind it is a salon, a coterie, a quarter of the town, or some single city; but Don Juan found his world in himself.

This model of grace and dignity, this captivating wit, moored his bark by every shore; but wherever he was led he was never carried away, and was only steered in a course of his own choosing. The more he saw, the more he doubted.

He watched men narrowly, and saw how, beneath the surface, courage was often rashness; and prudence, cowardice; generosity, a clever piece of calculation; justice, a wrong; delicacy, pusillanimity; honesty, a *modus vivendi*; and by some strange dispensation of fate, he must see that those who at heart were really honest, scrupulous, just, generous, prudent, or brave were held cheaply by their fellow-men.

"What a cold-blooded jest!" said he to himself. "It was not devised by a God."

From that time forth he renounced a better world, and never uncovered himself when a Name was pronounced, and for him the carven saints in the churches became works of art. He understood the mechanism of society too well to clash wantonly with its prejudices; for, after all, he was not as powerful as the executioner, but he evaded social laws with the wit and grace so well rendered in the scene with M. Dimanche. He was, in fact, Moliere's Don Juan, Goethe's Faust, Byron's Manfred, Mathurin's Melmoth—great allegorical figures drawn by the greatest men of genius in Europe, to which Mozart's harmonies, perhaps, do no more justice than Rossini's lyre. Terrible allegorical figures that shall endure as long as the principle of evil existing in the heart of man shall produce a few copies from century to century. Sometimes the type becomes half-human when incarnate as a Mirabeau, sometimes it is an inarticulate force in a Bonaparte, sometimes it overwhelms the universe with irony as a Rabelais; or, yet again, it appears when a Marechal de Richelieu elects to laugh at human beings instead of scoffing at things, or when one of the most famous of our ambassadors goes a step further and scoffs at both men and things. But the profound genius of Juan Belvidero anticipated and resumed all these. All things were a jest to him. His was the life of a mocking spirit. All men, all institutions, all realities, all ideas were within its scope. As for eternity, after half an hour of familiar conversation with Pope Julius II. he said, laughing:

"If it is absolutely necessary to make a choice, I would rather believe in God than in the Devil; power combined with goodness always offers more resources than the spirit of Evil can boast."

"Yes; still God requires repentance in this present world——"

"So you always think of your indulgences," returned Don Juan Belvidero. "Well, well, I have another life in reserve in which to repent of the sins of my previous existence."

"Oh, if you regard old age in that light," cried the Pope, "you are in danger on canonization——"

"After your elevation to the Papacy nothing is incredible." And they went to watch the workmen who were building the huge basilica dedicated to Saint Peter.

"Saint Peter, as the man of genius who laid the foundation of our double power," the Pope said to Don Juan, "deserves this monument. Sometimes, though, at night, I think that a deluge will wipe all this out as with a sponge, and it will be all to begin over again."

Don Juan and the Pope began to laugh; they understood each other. A fool would have gone on the morrow to amuse himself with Julius II. in Raphael's studio or at the delicious Villa Madama; not so Belvidero. He went to see the Pope as pontiff, to be convinced of any doubts that he (Don Juan) entertained. Over his cups the Rovere would have been capable of denying his own infallibility and of commenting on the Apocalypse.

Nevertheless, this legend has not been undertaken to furnish materials for future biographies of Don Juan; it is intended to prove to honest folk that Belvidero did not die in a duel with stone, as some lithographers would have us believe.

When Don Juan Belvidero reached the age of sixty he settled in Spain, and there in his old age he married a young and charming Andalusian wife. But of set purpose he was neither a good husband nor a good father. He had observed that we are never so tenderly loved as by women to whom we scarcely give a thought. Dona Elvira had been devoutly brought up by an old aunt in a castle a few leagues from San-

Lucar in a remote part of Andalusia. She was a model of devotion and grace. Don Juan foresaw that this would be a woman who would struggle long against a passion before yielding, and therefore hoped to keep her virtuous until his death. It was a jest undertaken in earnest, a game of chess which he meant to reserve till his old age. Don Juan had learned wisdom from the mistakes made by his father Bartolommeo; he determined that the least details of his life in old age should be subordinated to one object—the success of the drama which was to be played out upon his death-bed.

For the same reason the largest part of his wealth was buried in the cellars of his palace at Ferrara, whither he seldom went. As for the rest of his fortune, it was invested in a life annuity, with a view to give his wife and children an interest in keeping him alive; but this Machiavellian piece of foresight was scarcely necessary. His son, young Felipe Belvidero, grew up as a Spaniard as religiously conscientious as his father was irreligious, in virtue, perhaps, of the old rule, "A miser has a spendthrift son." The Abbot of San-Lucar was chosen by Don Juan to be the director of the consciences of the Duchess of Belvidero and her son Felipe. The ecclesiastic was a holy man, well shaped, and admirably well proportioned. He had fine dark eyes, a head like that of Tiberius, worn with fasting, bleached by an ascetic life, and, like all dwellers in the wilderness, was daily tempted. The noble lord had hopes, it may be, of despatching yet another monk before his term of life was out.

But whether because the Abbot was every whit as clever as Don Juan himself, or Dona Elvira possessed more discretion or more virtue than Spanish wives are usually credited with, Don Juan was compelled to spend his declining years beneath his own roof, with no more scandal under it than if he had been an ancient country parson. Occasionally he would take wife and son to task for negligence in the duties of religion, peremptorily insisting that they should carry out to the letter the obligations imposed upon the flock by the Court of Rome. Indeed, he was never so well pleased as when he had set the courtly Abbot discussing some case of conscience with Dona Elvira and Felipe.

At length, however, despite the prodigious care that the great magnifico, Don Juan Belvidero, took of himself, the days of decrepitude came upon him, and with those days the constant importunity of physical feebleness, an importunity all the more distressing by contrast with the wealth of memories of his impetuous youth and the sensual pleasures of middle age. The unbeliever who in the height of his cynical humor had been wont to persuade others to believe in laws and principles at which he scoffed, must repose nightly upon a *perhaps*. The great Duke, the pattern of good breeding, the champion of many a carouse, the proud ornament of Courts, the man of genius, the graceful winner of hearts that he had wrung as carelessly as a peasant twists an osier withe, was now the victim of a cough, of a ruthless sciatica, of an unmannerly gout. His teeth gradually deserted him, as at the end of an evening the fairest and best-dressed women take their leave one by one till the room is left empty and desolate. The active hands became palsy-stricken, the shapely legs tottered as he walked. At last, one night, a stroke of apoplexy caught him by the throat in its icy clutch. After that fatal day he grew morose and stern.

He would reproach his wife and son with their devotion, casting it in their teeth that the affecting and thoughtful care that they lavished so tenderly upon him was bestowed because they knew that his money was invested in a life annuity. Then Elvira and Felipe would shed bitter tears and redouble their caresses, and the wicked old man's insinuating voice would take an affectionate tone—"Ah, you will forgive me, will you not, dear friends, dear wife? I am rather a nuisance. Alas, Lord in heaven, how canst Thou use me as the instrument by which Thou provest these two angelic creatures? I who should be the joy of their lives am become their scourge..."

In this manner he kept them tethered to his pillow, blotting out the memory of whole months of fretfulness and unkindness in one short hour when he chose to display for them the ever-new treasures of his pinchbeck tenderness and charm of manner—a system of paternity that yielded him an infinitely better return than his own father's indulgence had formerly gained. At length his bodily infirmities reached a point when the task of laying him in bed became as difficult as the navigation of a felucca in the perils of an intricate channel. Then came the day of his death; and this brilliant sceptic, whose mental faculties alone had survived the most dreadful of all destructions, found himself between his two special antipathies—the doctor and the confessor. But he was jovial with them. Did he not see a light gleaming in the future beyond the veil? The pall that is like lead for other men was thin and translucent for him; the light-footed, irresistible delights of youth danced beyond it like shadows.

It was on a beautiful summer evening that Don Juan felt the near approach of death. The sky of Spain was serene and cloudless; the air was full of the scent of orange-blossom; the stars shed clear, pure gleams of light; nature without seemed to give the dying man assurance of resurrection; a dutiful and obedient son sat there watching him with loving and respectful eyes. Towards eleven o'clock he desired to be left alone with this single-hearted being.

"Felipe," said the father, in tones so soft and affectionate that the young man trembled, and tears of gladness came to his eyes; never had that stern father spoken his name in such a tone. "Listen, my son," the dying man went on. "I am a great sinner. All my life long, however, I have thought of my death.

I was once the friend of the great Pope Julius II.; and that illustrious Pontiff, fearing lest the excessive excitability of my senses should entangle me in mortal sin between the moment of my death and the time of my anointing with the holy oil, gave me a flask that contains a little of the holy water that once issued from the rock in the wilderness. I have kept the secret of this squandering of a treasure belonging to Holy Church, but I am permitted to reveal the mystery *in articulo mortis* to my son. You will find the flask in a drawer in that Gothic table that always stands by the head of the bed.... The precious little crystal flask may be of use yet again for you, dearest Felipe. Will you swear to me, by your salvation, to carry out my instructions faithfully?"

Felipe looked at his father, and Don Juan was too deeply learned in the lore of the human countenance not to die in peace with that look as his warrant, as his own father had died in despair at meeting the expression in his son's eyes.

"You deserved to have a better father," Don Juan went on. "I dare to confess, my child, that while the reverend Abbot of San-Lucar was administering the Viaticum I was thinking of the incompatibility of the co-existence of two powers so infinite as God and the Devil——"

"Oh, father!"

"And I said to myself, when Satan makes his peace he ought surely to stipulate for the pardon of his followers, or he will be the veriest scoundrel. The thought haunted me; so I shall go to hell, my son, unless you carry out my wishes."

"Oh, quick; tell me quickly, father."

"As soon as I have closed my eyes," Don Juan went on, "and that may be in a few minutes, you must take my body before it grows cold and lay it on a table in this room. Then put out the lamp; the light of the stars should be sufficient. Take off my clothes, reciting Aves and Paters the while, raising your soul to God in prayer, and carefully anoint my lips and eyes with this holy water; begin with the face, and proceed successively to my limbs and the rest of my body; my dear son, the power of God is so great that you must be astonished at nothing."

Don Juan felt death so near, that he added in a terrible voice, "Be careful not to drop the flask."

Then he breathed his last gently in the arms of his son, and his son's tears fell fast over his sardonic, haggard features.

It was almost midnight when Don Felipe Belvidero laid his father's body upon the table. He kissed the sinister brow and the gray hair; then he put out the lamp.

By the soft moonlight that lit strange gleams across the country without, Felipe could dimly see his father's body, a vague white thing among the shadows. The dutiful son moistened a linen cloth with the liquid, and, absorbed in prayer, he anointed the revered face. A deep silence reigned. Felipe heard faint, indescribable rustlings; it was the breeze in the tree-tops, he thought. But when he had moistened the right arm, he felt himself caught by the throat, a young strong hand held him in a tight grip—it was his father's hand! He shrieked aloud; the flask dropped from his hand and broke in pieces. The liquid evaporated; the whole household hurried into the room, holding torches aloft. That shriek had startled them, and filled them with as much terror as if the Trumpet of the Angel sounding on the Last Day had rung through earth and sky. The room was full of people, and a horror-stricken crowd beheld the fainting Felipe upheld by the strong arm of his father, who clutched him by the throat. They saw another thing, an unearthly spectacle—Don Juan's face grown young and beautiful as Antinous, with its dark hair and brilliant eyes and red lips, a head that made horrible efforts, but could not move the dead, wasted body.

An old servitor cried, "A miracle! a miracle!" and all the Spaniards echoed, "A miracle! a miracle!"

Dona Elvira, too pious to attribute this to magic, sent for the Abbot of San-Lucar; and the Prior beholding the miracle with his own eyes, being a clever man, and withal an Abbot desirous of augmenting his revenues, determined to turn the occasion to profit. He immediately gave out that Don Juan would certainly be canonized; he appointed a day for the celebration of the apotheosis in his convent, which thenceforward, he said, should be called the convent of San Juan of Lucar. At these words a sufficiently facetious grimace passed over the features of the late Duke.

The taste of the Spanish people for ecclesiastical solemnities is so well known, that it should not be difficult to imagine the religious pantomime by which the Convent of San-Lucar celebrated the translation of the *blessed Don Juan Belvidero* to the abbey-church. The tale of the partial resurrection had spread so quickly from village to village, that a day or two after the death of the illustrious nobleman the report had reached every place within fifty miles of San-Lucar, and it was as good as a play to see the roads covered already with crowds flocking in on all sides, their curiosity whetted still further by the prospect of a *Te Deum* sung by torchlight. The old abbey church of San-Lucar, a marvelous building erected by the Moors, a mosque of Allah, which for three centuries had heard the name of Christ, could not hold the throng that poured in to see the ceremony. Hidalgos in their velvet mantles, with their good swords at their sides, swarmed like ants, and were so tightly packed in among the pillars that they had not room to bend the knees, which never bent save to God. Charming peasant girls, in the basquina that defines the luxuriant outlines of their figures, lent an arm to white-haired old men. Young men, with eyes of fire, walked beside aged crones in holiday array. Then came couples tremulous with joy, young lovers led thither by curiosity, newly-wedded folk; children timidly clasping each other by the hand. This throng, so rich in coloring, in vivid contrasts, laden with flowers, enameled like a meadow, sent up a soft murmur through the quiet night. Then the great doors of the church opened.

Late comers who remained without saw afar, through the three great open doorways, a scene of which the theatrical illusions of modern opera can give but a faint idea. The vast church was lighted up by thousands of candles, offered by saints and sinners alike eager to win the favor of this new candidate for canonization, and these self-commending illuminations turned the great building into an enchanted fairyland. The black archways, the shafts and capitals, the recessed chapels with gold and silver gleaming in their depths, the galleries, the Arab traceries, all the most delicate outlines of that delicate sculpture, burned in the excess of light like the fantastic figures in the red heart of a brazier. At the further end of the church, above that blazing sea, rose the high altar like a splendid dawn. All the glories of the golden lamps and silver candlesticks, of banners and tassels, of the shrines of the saints and votive offerings, paled before the gorgeous brightness of the reliquary in which Don Juan lay. The blasphemer's body sparkled with gems, and flowers, and crystal, with diamonds and gold, and plumes white as the wings of seraphim; they had set it up on the altar, where the pictures of Christ had stood. All about him blazed a host of tall candles; the air quivered in the radiant light. The worthy Abbot of San-Lucar, in pontifical robes, with his mitre set with precious stones, his rochet and golden crosier, sat enthroned in imperial state among his clergy in the choir. Rows of impassive aged faces, silver-haired old men clad in fine linen albs, were grouped about him, as the saints who confessed Christ on earth are set by painters, each in his place, about the throne of God in heaven. The precentor and the dignitaries of the chapter, adorned with the gorgeous insignia of ecclesiastical vanity, came and went through the clouds of incense, like stars upon their courses in the firmament.

When the hour of triumph arrived, the bells awoke the echoes far and wide, and the whole vast crowd raised to God the first cry of praise that begins the *Te Deum*. A sublime cry! High, pure notes, the voices of women in ecstasy, mingled in it with the sterner and deeper voices of men; thousands of voices sent up a volume of sound so mighty, that the straining, groaning organ-pipes could not dominate that harmony. But the shrill sound of children's singing among the choristers, the reverberation of deep bass notes, awakened gracious associations, visions of childhood, and of man in his strength, and rose above that entrancing harmony of human voices blended in one sentiment of love.

Te Deum laudamus*!*

The chant went up from the black masses of men and women kneeling in the cathedral, like a sudden breaking out of light in darkness, and the silence was shattered as by a peal of thunder. The voices floated up with the clouds of incense that had begun to cast thin bluish veils over the fanciful marvels of the architecture, and the aisles were filled with splendor and perfume and light and melody. Even at the moment when that music of love and thanksgiving soared up to the altar, Don Juan, too well bred not to express his acknowledgments, too witty not to understand how to take a jest, bridled up in his reliquary, and responded with an appalling burst of laughter. Then the Devil having put him in mind of the risk he was running of being taken for an ordinary man, a saint, a Boniface, a Pantaleone, he interrupted the melody of love by a yell, the thousand voices of hell joined in it. Earth blessed, Heaven banned. The church was shaken to its ancient foundations.

Te Deum laudamus! cried the many voices.

"Go to the devil, brute beasts that you are! *Dios! Dios! Garajos demonios!* Idiots! What fools you are with your dotard God!" and a torrent of imprecations poured forth like a stream of red-hot lava from the mouth of Vesuvius.

"*Deus Sabaoth!... Sabaoth*!" cried the believers.

"You are insulting the majesty of Hell," shouted Don Juan, gnashing his teeth. In another moment the living arm struggled out of the reliquary, and was brandished over the assembly in mockery and despair.

"The saint is blessing us," cried the old women, children, lovers, and the credulous among the crowd.

And note how often we are deceived in the homage we pay; the great man scoffs at those who praise him, and pays compliments now and again to those whom he laughs at in the depths of his heart.

Just as the Abbot, prostrate before the altar, was chanting "*Sancte Johannes, ora pro noblis!*" he heard a voice exclaim sufficiently distinctly: "*O coglione!*"

"What can be going on up there?" cried the Sub-prior, as he saw the reliquary move.

"The saint is playing the devil," replied the Abbot.

Even as he spoke the living head tore itself away from the lifeless body, and dropped upon the sallow cranium of the officiating priest.

"Remember Dona Elvira!" cried the thing, with its teeth set fast in the Abbot's head.

The Abbot's horror-stricken shriek disturbed the ceremony; all the ecclesiastics hurried up and crowded about their chief.

"Idiot, tell us now if there is a God!" the voice cried, as the Abbot, bitten through the brain, drew his last breath.

PARIS, October 1830.

CONTENTS

PREPARER'S NOTE 3

THE NAPOLEON OF THE PEOPLE 4

   TO THE READER 35

THE ELIXIR OF LIFE 39